My Book of

FUNNY STORIES

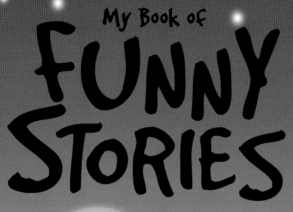

W

FRANKLIN WATTS

LONDON • SYDNEY

Contents

Jasper and Jess

by Anne Cassidy

Illustrated by François Hall

Jasper and Jess were enemies.

Jasper liked to chase Jess out of his garden.

Every day Jasper waited until

Jess appeared.

He chased her until she ran up

the apple tree.

He barked and growled at her.

She arched her back and
hissed at him.

One day Jess didn't appear.

Jasper looked for her behind the bushes and in the flowerbeds.

He looked in the rock garden ...

... and over the fence.

But Jess wasn't there.

Then Jasper heard a sound.

He looked up at the house.

Jess was stuck on the roof!

Jasper went to have a closer look.

Jess was hanging down from the drainpipe!

Jasper ran up and down the garden, barking.

But no one heard him.

He scratched at the back door.

But no one was at home.

Quickly, he pulled a deckchair under the drainpipe.

"Jump onto the chair, Jess!"

he shouted.

Jess was frightened but she closed her eyes and let go.

It was a long way down.

Jess fell through the air and landed on the chair.

She was safe!

Jasper was glad he had helped Jess.

Now he could chase her out of his garden again!

The cat that went Woof!

by Martyn Beardsley

Illustrated by Lisa Smith

Tiger lived with Jack.

They were the best of friends.

Then along came Patch.

Everything changed.

Everyone
laughed when
Patch barked.

They patted
his head
when he
wagged
his tail.

So Tiger decided she would learn to bark.

Then everyone would laugh and pat her head!

"WOOF!" said Tiger.

"Mum, I think Tiger's got a cough!" said Jack.

"WOOF! WOOF!" said Tiger when the post arrived.

"Mum, I think Tiger's swallowed a letter!" said Jack.

They took Tiger to see the vet.

"What's wrong?" asked the vet.

"She doesn't sound very well,"

said Jack.

"WOOF!" said Tiger.

"I see!" said the vet.

"Do you have any other pets?" asked the vet.

"A new puppy called Patch!"

said Jack.

"*I see!*" said the vet.

"Then plenty of love and stroking should solve the problem!" said the vet.

"MIAOW!" said Tiger.

"MIOOF!" said Patch.

Mary and the Fairy

by Penny Dolan

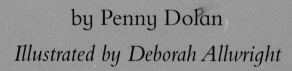

Illustrated by Deborah Allwright

A fairy flew in through

Mary's window.

"Mary, why are you so sad?" she asked.

"I've got nothing to wear to the party," Mary said.

The fairy smiled.

"Mary, you shall go to the Ball!"

she cried.

"Wait ..." stammered Mary.

But the fairy wasn't listening at all.

"How about a red frock?"

asked the fairy.

The red frock made Mary feel terribly hot.

"But ..." she said.

"Well, what about a blue frock?" asked the fairy.

The blue frock made Mary feel terribly glum.

"No!" she said.

"I know! A yellow frock!"

the fairy cried.

The yellow frock made Mary's eyes go terribly wiggly.

"I've got it this time! A green frock!" shouted the fairy.

The green frock made Mary's tummy feel terribly wobbly.

"Yuk!" she said.

"No, don't tell me ... you want a silver frock!" guessed the fairy.

The silver frock made Mary feel terribly shivery.

"Stop!" shouted Mary.

"What colour frock do you want?" said the fairy crossly.

"I haven't got all day, you know!"

"I don't want a frock," Mary sighed.

"What I really want, is ..."

"Oh, I see!" said the fairy.

She waved her wand again.

Pazazz!

"Is that right?" she asked.

"Oh, yes! Thank you, fairy," cried Mary.

"Now, I shall go to the
fancy dress party."

The Cheeky Monkey

by Anne Cassidy

Illustrated by Lisa Smith

Wendy woke up late one day.

She walked into the garden

and found ...

... a monkey sitting in
her treehouse.

"Monkey, get out of my treehouse!"

Wendy shouted.

"No, I'm staying here!" the monkey shouted back.

Wendy turned purple with anger.

"Oh no, you're not!" she shouted.

Wendy made a plan.

She went into battle with
the monkey.

But the monkey had custard pies.

"Take that!" he shouted as he threw them at Wendy.

Wendy needed a new plan.

She went to have a look in

her toy box.

Wendy became a pirate.

She was going to capture
the treehouse.

The monkey became a pirate, too.

He shot at Wendy with hundreds of peanuts.

So Wendy became a cowgirl.

She made a plan to capture
the monkey.

But the monkey had a better plan

and Wendy got very wet.

The monkey laughed and laughed.

Wendy made another plan.
She went into the kitchen.

Wendy made a trap for the monkey.
He came straight down from
the treehouse ...

... and got straight into

Wendy's bed!

Croc's Tooth

by Anne Cassidy

Illustrated by Mike Phillips

Croc wanted to play,
but he had a bad tooth.
"Help me, Hippo," he said.

Hippo grabbed hold of
Croc's tooth.

She pulled and pulled.

The tooth wouldn't come out.

Hippo tied a rope to the tooth.

Then she swam as fast as she could.

Still the tooth wouldn't come out.

Next Croc climbed up the river bank.
Hippo pushed a rock up
to the top.

Hippo tied one end of the rope to Croc's tooth and the other to the rock ...

then she dropped

the rock!

Still the tooth wouldn't come out.

"You need to see a dentist!"

Hippo said.

Croc and Hippo got a lift behind a boat.

They walked through the town.

Hippo saw a policeman. She asked him where they could find a dentist.

"Over there," he said.

Dentist

Croc and Hippo sat and waited.

The dentist said, "Next, please!"

Croc climbed in the chair.

"What can I do for you, Mr ...?"

The dentist jumped.

He screamed!

Then he looked at the tooth. The dentist was gentle.

He pulled the tooth and out it came.

Now Croc is happy.

He can play with Hippo again!

The Animals' Football Cup

by Clare De Marco

Illustrated by Trevor Dunton

It was the day of the football cup final.

Jungle United were excited.

"I'm fierce!" roared Lion.

"I'll stop the other team."

"I'm tall," said Giraffe.

"I'll head the ball into the goal."

"I'm nimble," said Gazelle.
"I'll kick the ball to Giraffe."

Hippo said nothing.

"I'm not good at anything,"

he thought.

The Rainforest Rovers team arrived.

They were fast and strong.

RAINFOREST
ROVERS

Monkey blew his whistle

to start the game.

Hippo didn't play well.

First, he stood on Giraffe.

Then Hippo scored an
own goal by mistake.

“0-1 to Rainforest Rovers!”

shouted Monkey.

"I'm too big and clumsy,"

thought Hippo, sadly.

Gazelle had an idea.

"You're big," she said.

"You can be the goalkeeper!"

Hippo smiled.

Soon Lion roared past the other team and scored.

"1-1!" shouted Monkey.

Then Gazelle kicked the ball high
and Giraffe headed it in.

"2-1 to Jungle United!" shouted Monkey.

But in the last minute, Lion tripped up a Rainforest Rovers player.

"Penalty!" shouted Monkey.

Hippo shook in his goal as the player ran up to take the penalty …

… but the ball bounced straight off

Hippo's bottom!

Monkey blew his whistle.

"Jungle United win!"

"Three cheers for Hippo!"

Bill's Baggy Trousers

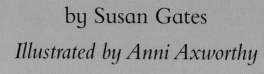

by Susan Gates

Illustrated by Anni Axworthy

Bill's mum bought him some

new trousers.

The trousers
were very big
and baggy.

They had
lots of
pockets.

Bill's mum sent him to the shops.

"I can put the shopping in my pockets," said Bill.

"I'd like some potatoes, please," said Bill to the shopkeeper.

The shopkeeper helped Bill
fill his pockets with the potatoes.

IT VEG

"I can't walk!" said Bill. "My trousers are much too heavy."

Bill took all the potatoes

out of his pockets.

Suddenly, the wind began to blow up Bill's trousers.

They got bigger and bigger

and bigger.

"Oh no!" shouted Bill.

"I'm floating away!"

Bill floated high up into the sky.

He floated over the town ...

and waved to his mum in the garden.

Bill's mum didn't see him.

"Look at me, Mum!" shouted Bill.

Suddenly, a bird pecked Bill's trousers.

They went Sssssssssss ...

Bill's trousers got smaller and smaller.

"Look out! I'm coming down,"

he shouted.

Bill landed next to his mum in the garden.

"You were quick!" she said.

Hannibal's Noisy Day

by Anne Adeney

Illustrated by Christina Bretschneider

It was morning.

Hannibal the hamster shut his eyes.

"It's time for me to sleep now."

Squeak!

Then Jacob's alarm clock rang:

COCK-A-DOODLE-DOOOO!

"Be quiet!" said Hannibal.

"I'm trying to sleep!"

“Jacob is going to school,” said Hannibal.

“Time for me to sleep.”

Then the postman arrived: DING-DONG!

"Be quiet!" said Hannibal. "I'm trying to sleep!"

Hannibal shut his eyes.

Then Grandma started cleaning:

BRMM-BRMM!

"Be quiet!" said Hannibal.

"I'm trying to sleep!"

Hannibal went to sleep.

Then the baby started to cry:

"WAAH-WAAH!"

"Be quiet!" said Hannibal.

"I'm trying to sleep!"

"I'll sleep now," said Hannibal.

An ambulance went by:

NEE-NAA! NEE-NAA!

"Be quiet!" said Hannibal.

"I'm trying to sleep!"

Later on, Kelly came in.

"Wake up, Hannibal!" said Kelly.

"Let's play!"

"Be quiet!" said Hannibal.

"I'm trying to sleep!"

When Dad came home, he cut the grass:

Then Mum put the radio on:

"LA-LA-LA-LA-LAAAA!"

"BE QUIET!" said Hannibal.

"I'm trying to sleep.

Why are you so noisy?"

At last, everyone sat down to eat.

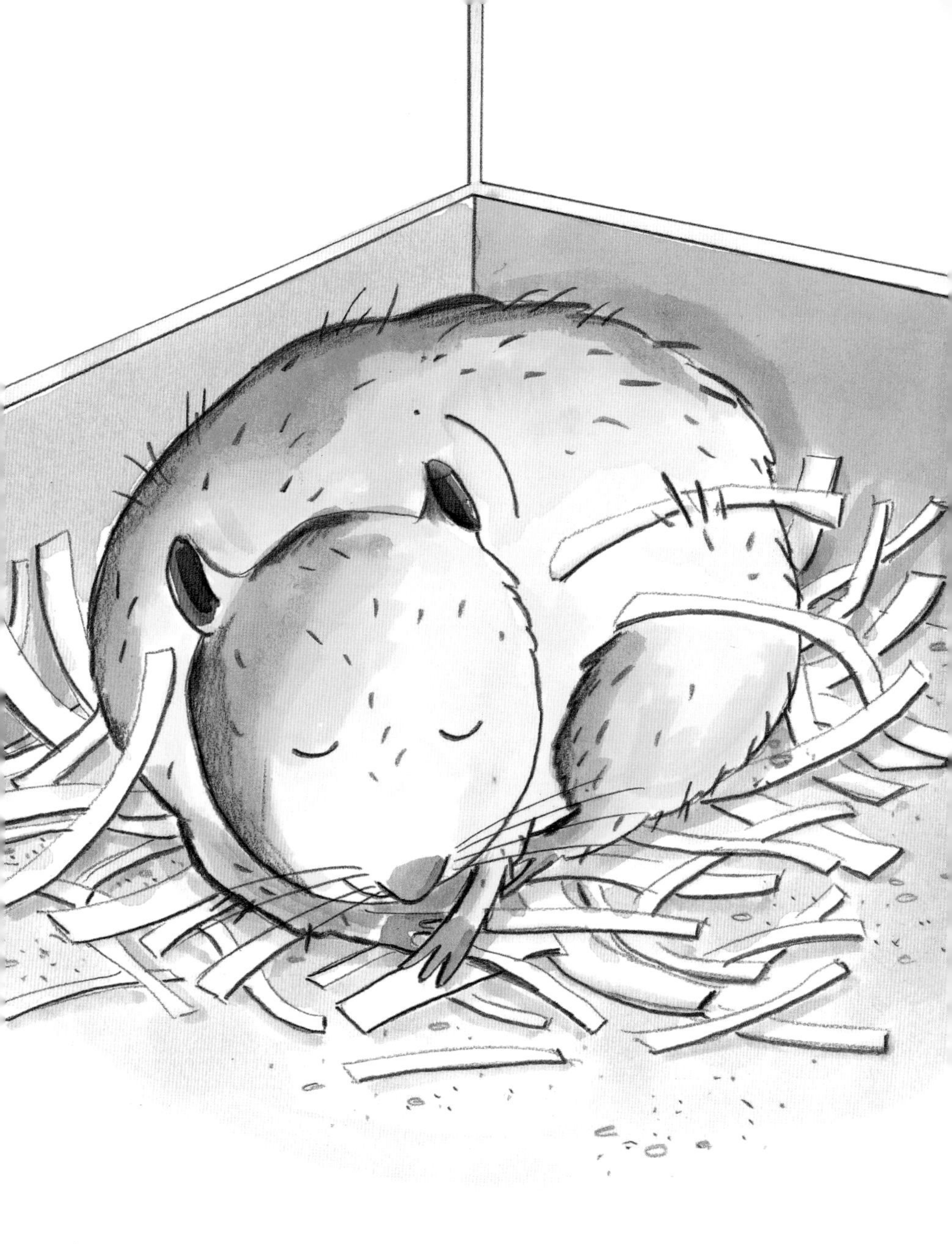

Hannibal could have a good sleep.

When Hannibal woke up,

he saw his wheel.

"*I* can play now," he said:

CLITTER-CLATTER!

Be quiet, Hannibal! We're trying to sleep!

Waah!

The Queen, the Mice and the Cheese

by Carrie Weston

Illustrated by Martin Remphry

Once there was a queen who lived in a splendid palace.

She loved her rich furniture …

she loved her fine clothes …

she loved her beautiful garden.

But most of all, the queen

loved cheese.

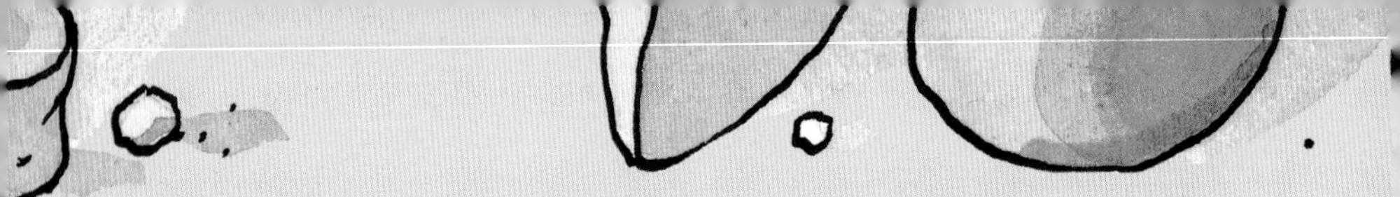

The royal kitchen was full of cheese.

There was hard cheese …

and soft cheese …

and blue cheese.

There was even cheese with holes in.

It was not just the queen who loved cheese. All the mice in the land loved cheese, too. Before long, they started to visit the palace.

Soon there were mice in
the cupboards …

under the table …

and even mice on
the royal throne.

The queen threw up her hands in horror. She called for her ministers. "Cats!" they said, nodding wisely. "Send for some cats!"

So all the cats in the land were invited to the palace to chase away the mice. And they did.

When the mice were gone, the cats made themselves at home.

They dozed on the royal bed …

and sharpened their claws on the throne.

The queen was horrified.

She called for her ministers again.

"Dogs!" they said at last. "Send for some dogs to chase away the cats."

All the dogs in the land were invited to the royal palace. The dogs quickly chased away the cats.

Then the dogs made themselves at home. They chewed up the queen's slippers.

They buried bones in the royal gardens.

"Enough!" cried the queen in despair.

"Where are my ministers?"

The ministers sat around and scratched their heads. At last, they had an answer. "Elephants!" they cried. "Bring in some elephants."

Soon the palace was full of elephants. When the dogs saw them, they ran away as fast as they could.

The elephants loved their new home.

They squashed the sofas.

They splashed in the pond.

And they were far too big to squeeze through the doors. "Oh, my splendid palace!" yelled the queen.

The ministers came at once.

They looked in big books.

Then they all nodded wisely.

“We have an answer!” they said.

"Mice!" announced the ministers.

"Elephants are afraid of mice!"

The ministers were very pleased with themselves.

The queen was not quite so pleased, but she had an idea. First, she watched as the mice chased all the elephants out of the palace.

Then the queen called the mice to her meeting room. The queen made two rules.

1. Mice may only eat cheese labelled "Cheese for mice."
2. Mice will not bring cats, dogs, or elephants to the palace.

The mice chatted amongst themselves. Then they nodded and signed the queen's rules.

When the builders had finished,
the queen once again lived in
a splendid palace.

And she was very happy to share her cheese with the mice – just as long as they kept to the rules!

Felix on the Move

by Maeve Friel

Illustrated by Beccy Blake

Felix was a very happy cat.

He liked sitting on the window sill ...

… and napping in secret places.

He liked playing in the garden.

And he liked his family so much,

he gave them a present every day.

One morning, a big van arrived at the house.

Out went the sofa where Felix liked to have his afternoon naps.

Out went the rug that he sharpened his claws on.

Out went the beds, the television and the fridge.

Worst of all, out went his yellow, plastic bowl.

Felix was not a happy cat.

Soon, there was nothing left but a cat basket.

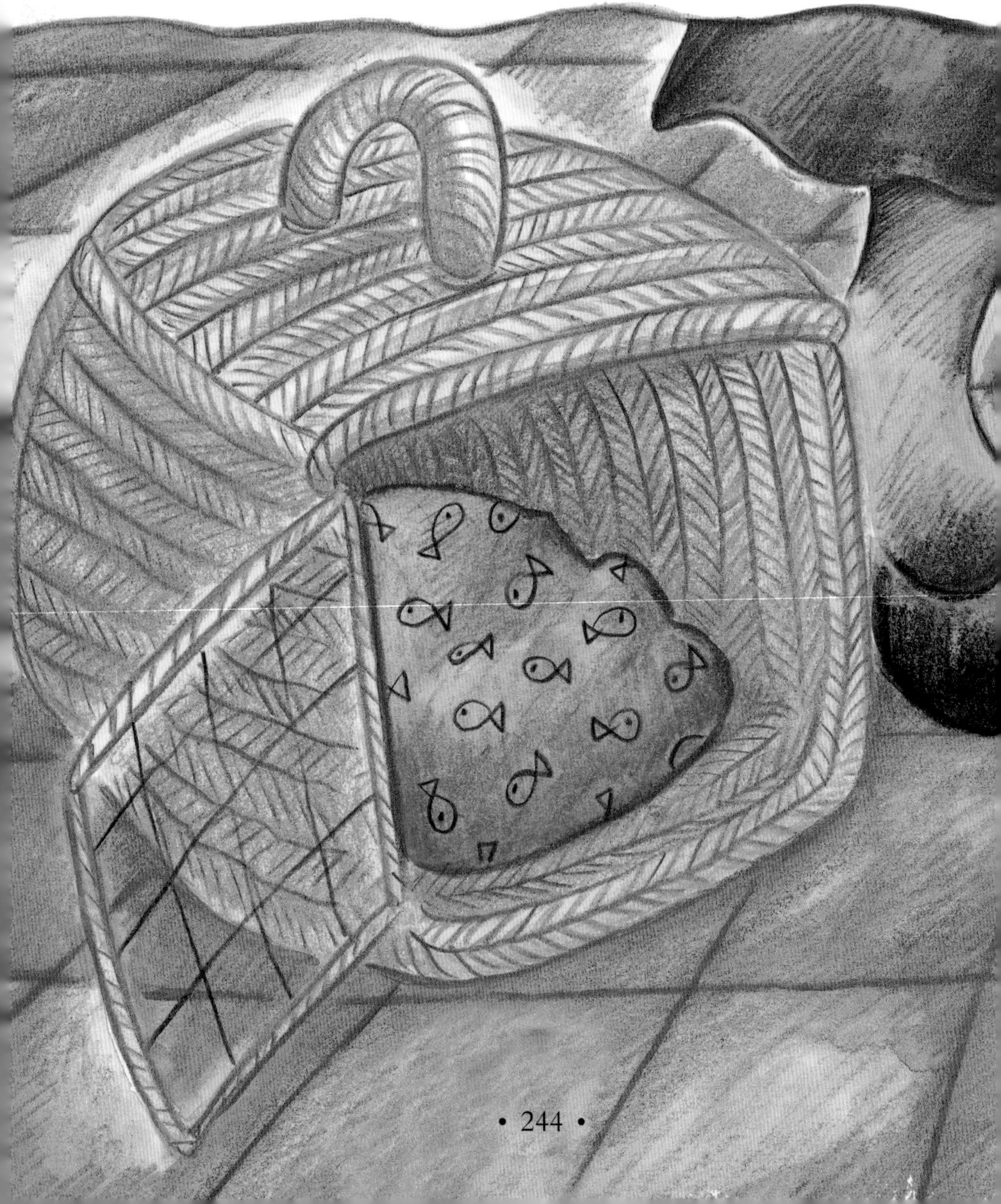

"I'm not getting in that," growled Felix.

But he did!

Felix was all alone in an empty room.

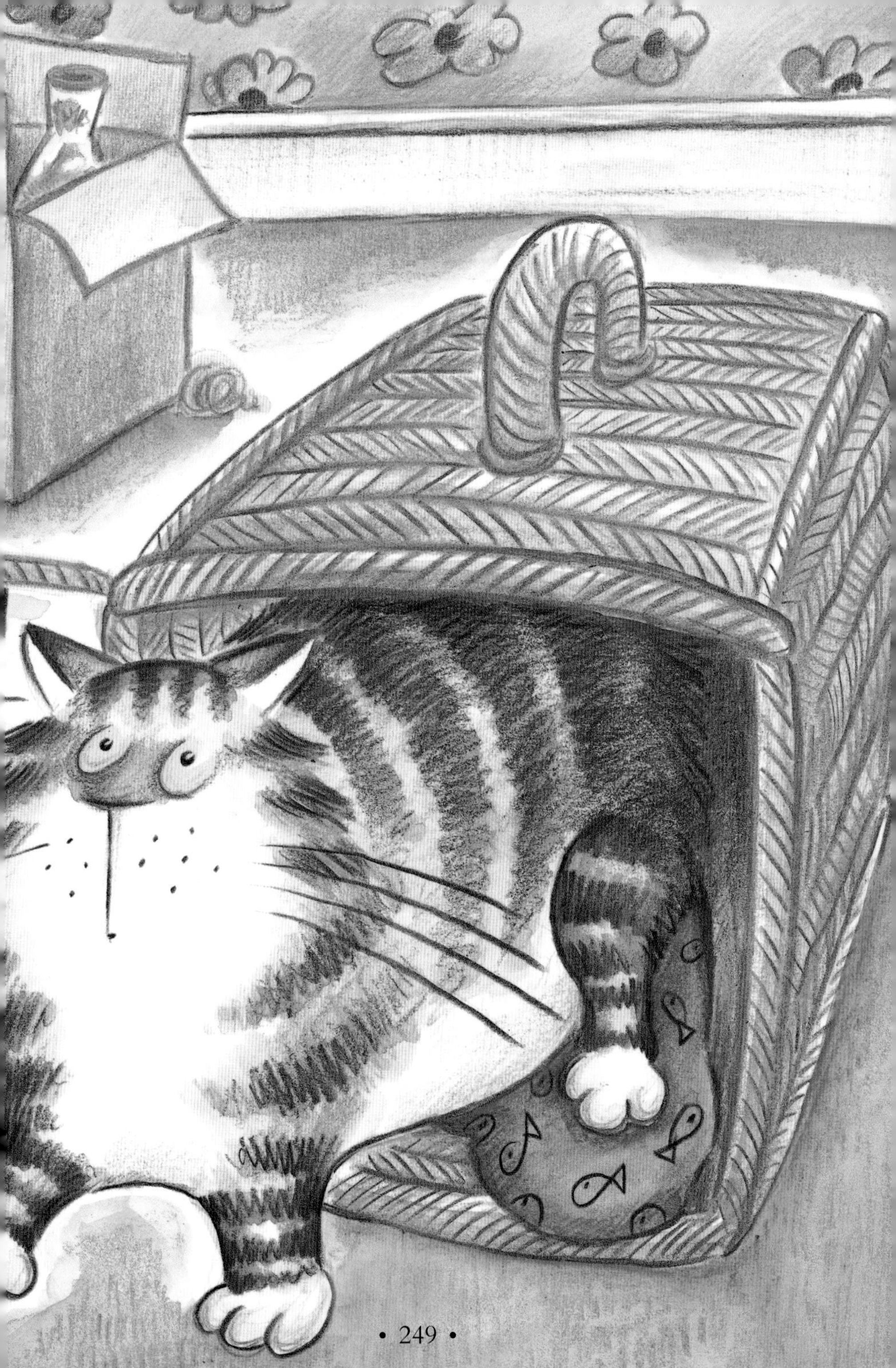

In came the sofa, the rug, the television and the fridge.

In came his yellow, plastic bowl.

Best of all, in came the family.

Felix was a very happy cat.

First published in 2014 by
Franklin Watts
338 Euston Road
London NW1 3BH

Franklin Watts Australia
Level 17/207 Kent Street
Sydney NSW 2000

The author and illustrator acknowledgements on pages 4, 26, 50, 74, 100, 126, 154, 178, 202, 230 consititute an extension of this copyright page.

A CIP catalogue record for this book is available from the British Library.

ISBN 978 1 4451 2736 1

Editor: Jackie Hamley
Designer: Chris Fraser
Cover designer: Cathryn Gilbert

Printed in China

Franklin Watts is a division of Hachette Children's Books, an Hachette UK company.

www.hachette.co.uk